HUSH
LITTLE
DIGGER

by Ellen Olson-Brown

Illustrations by Lee White

I hope you "dig" this book, Lars! ♡, Ellen Olson-Brown

TRICYCLE PRESS
Berkeley/Toronto

Hush, little digger, don't say a word,
Papa's gonna scoop you a pile of dirt.

And if that dirt starts to overflow,

Papa's gonna find you a red backhoe.

And if that backhoe has a bad motor,

Papa's gonna find you a front-end loader.

And if that loader runs into bad luck,

Papa's gonna find you a big dump truck.

And if that dump truck shakes,
quiver-quaver,

Papa's gonna find you an asphalt paver.

And if that paver hits a rock that slows her,

Papa's gonna find you a yellow bulldozer.

And if that 'dozer springs an oil gusher,

Papa's gonna find you a concrete crusher.

And if that crusher's lights blink and flicker,

Papa's gonna find you a cherry picker.

And if that picker can't stay still,

Papa's gonna find you an auger drill.

And if that drill just won't
drive deeper,

Papa's gonna find you a green street sweeper.

And while that sweeper cleans the town,

You'll still be the best little digger around.

To the three construction guys I dig the most,
Milo, Cyrus, and Caleb   —E.O.B.

To my Team Anonymous wrecking crew,
Brian and Paul   —L.W.

Text copyright © 2006 by Ellen Olson-Brown
Illustrations copyright © 2006 by Lee White

Tricycle Press
an imprint of Ten Speed Press
P.O. Box 7123
Berkeley, California 94707
www.tricyclepress.com

Design by Betsy Stromberg
Typeset in Domestos
The illustrations in this book were painted in oil
    and colored pencil.

Library of Congress Cataloging-in-Publication Data

Olson-Brown, Ellen, 1967-
  Hush, little digger / by Ellen Olson-Brown ;
illustrations by Lee White.
     p. cm.
  Summary: In this variation of the classic lullaby, a
father reassures his son that the boy is better than a
dump truck, a backhoe, or even a bulldozer when it
comes to digging.
  ISBN-13: 978-1-58246-160-1
  ISBN-10: 1-58246-160-0
 1. Folk songs, English--Texts. [1. Lullabies. 2. Folk
songs.] I. White, Lee, 1970- ill. II. Title.
  PZ8.3.O4988Hus 2006
  782.42--dc22

                                    2005021959

First Tricycle Press printing, 2006
Printed in China

2 3 4 5 6 — 10 09 08 07 06